JUL '07

A Note to Parents and Caregivers:

Read-it! Joke Books are for children who are moving ahead on the amazing road to reading. These fun books support the acquisition and extension of reading skills as well as a love of books.

Published by the same company that produces *Read-it!* Readers, these books introduce the question/answer and dialogue patterns that help children expand their thinking about language structure and book formats.

When sharing joke books with a child, read in short stretches. Pause often to talk about the meaning of the jokes. The question/answer and dialogue formats work well for this purpose and provide an opportunity to talk about the language and meaning of the jokes. Have the child turn the pages and point to the pictures and familiar words. When you read the jokes, have fun creating the voices of characters or emphasizing some important words. Be sure to reread favorite jokes.

There is no right or wrong way to share books with children. Find time to read with your child, and pass on the legacy of literacy.

Adria F. Klein, Ph.D.
Professor Emeritus
California State University
San Bernardino, California

Editor: Christianne Jones
Designer: Joe Anderson
Creative Director: Keith Griffin
Editorial Director: Carol Jones
Managing Editor: Catherine Neitge
Page Production: Picture Window Books
The illustrations in this book were created digitally.

Picture Window Books
5115 Excelsior Boulevard
Suite 232
Minneapolis, MN 55416
877-845-8392
www.picturewindowbooks.com

Printed in the United States of America.

Library of Congress Cataloging-in-Publication Data
Ziegler, Mark, 1954-
Chitchat chuckles : a book of funny talk / by Mark Ziegler ; illustrated by
Ryan Haugen.
p. cm. – (Read-it! joke books—supercharged!)
ISBN 1-4048-1160-5 (hardcover)
1. Wit and humor, Juvenile. I. Haugen, Ryan, 1972- II. Title. III. Series.

PN6166.Z54 2006
818'.602–dc22   2005004067

Chitchat Chuckles

A Book of Funny Talk

by Mark Ziegler   illustrated by Ryan Haugen

Special thanks to our advisers for their expertise:

Adria F. Klein, Ph.D.
Professor Emeritus, California State University
San Bernardino, California

Susan Kesselring, M.A.
Literacy Educator
Rosemount–Apple Valley–Eagan (Minnesota) School District

PICTURE WINDOW BOOKS
Minneapolis, Minnesota

What did the sock say to the foot?
"You're putting me on!"

**What did the second-hand say
to the number twelve?**
"I'll be back in a minute."

What did one cowboy say to the other cowboy while they were rounding up cattle?
"Stop me if you already 'herd' this one."

What did the nose say to the finger?
"Pick on someone your own size!"

What did the egg say to the stand-up comic?
"You crack me up!"

What did the blanket say to the bed?
"Don't worry, I've got you covered."

What did the duck say when it bought some lipstick?
"Put it on my bill."

What did one raindrop say to the other?
"Two's company, three's a cloud."

**What did the big chimney say
to the little chimney?**
"You're too young to smoke."

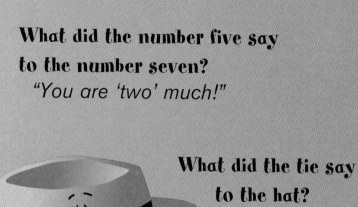

What did the number five say to the number seven?
"You are 'two' much!"

What did the tie say to the hat?
"You go on a head, and I'll hang around here for awhile."

**What do volcanoes say
on Valentine's Day?**
  "I lava you!"

What did one tonsil say to the other?
  *"Get dressed up! A doctor is
  taking us out."*

What did the police officer
say to his stomach?
"You're under a vest!"

What did the doe say
to her little fawn?
"Hello, 'deer.'"

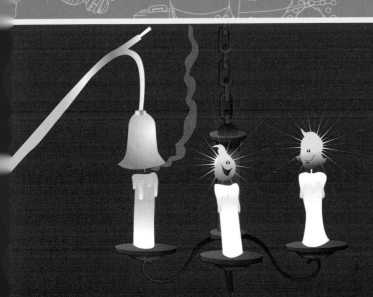

**What did one candle say
to the other candle?**
"Let's go out tonight!"

**What did the farmer say after
he dug two holes in the ground?**
"Well, well."

**What did the magician say when the
left side of his body disappeared?**
"I'm all right now."

What did the woodpecker say to the ghost?
"You scared the peck out of me!"

What did one angel say to the other angel?
"Halo!"

What did the cherry say when
it was made into jam?
"This is the pits!"

What did the nut say
when it sneezed?
"Cashew!"

What did the stamp
say to the envelope?
"Stick with me, and we'll
go places."

What did the hammer
say to the board?
"I just broke a nail!"

14

What did the baby porcupine
say to the pin cushion?
 "Mommy!"

What did the nose say to the eyes?
 "Sorry, but I gotta run!"

What did the hair say
to the comb?
 *"Nothing can
keep us
a part."*

What did the astronomer
say to the telescope?
"Business is looking up."

What does Santa say when he
works in his garden?
"'Hoe,' 'hoe,' 'hoe!'"

**What did one flea say
to the other flea?**
"Shall we walk or take
the greyhound?"

**What did the bus driver
say to the kangaroo?**
"Hop in."

What did the dirt say to the rain?
"Thanks to you, my name is mud!"

What did the mama cow say to her calf one night?
"Pasture bed time, isn't it?"

What did the Egyptian say after he prepared a mummy?
"That's a wrap!"

**What did the mother earthworm
say to her little earthworm?**
  "Where in earth have you been?"

What did one spider say to the other?
  "See you on the web."

What did the computer say to the virus?
"Stop bugging me!"

What did the mayonnaise say to the refrigerator?
"Close the door! I'm dressing!"

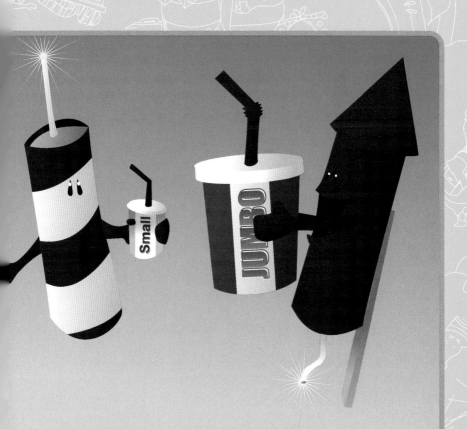

What did one firecracker say to the other?
"My pop is bigger than your pop!"

What did one elevator say to the other elevator?
"I think I'm coming down with something."

What did the mother horse say to the mother goat?
  "How are the kids?"

What did the invisible man's girlfriend say to him?
  "I can't see you anymore."

What did the bee say to the flower?
  "Hey, bud, when do you open up?"

What did the beaver say to the oak tree?
"Been nice gnawing you."

What did the ram say to his girlfriend?
"I like 'ewe.'"

Read-it! Joke Books— Supercharged!

Beastly Laughs: A Book of Monster Jokes by Michael Dahl

Chalkboard Chuckles: A Book of Classroom Jokes by Mark Moore

Creepy Crawlers: A Book of Bug Jokes by Mark Moore

Critter Jitters: A Book of Animal Jokes by Mark Ziegler

Fur, Feathers, and Fun! A Book of Animal Jokes by Mark Ziegler

Giggle Bubbles: A Book of Underwater Jokes by Mark Ziegler

Goofballs! A Book of Sports Jokes by Mark Ziegler

Lunchbox Laughs: A Book of Food Jokes by Mark Ziegler

Mind Knots: A Book of Riddles by Mark Ziegler

Nutty Names: A Book of Name Jokes by Mark Ziegler

Roaring with Laughter: A Book of Animal Jokes by Michael Dahl

School Kidders: A Book of School Jokes by Mark Ziegler

Sit! Stay! Laugh! A Book of Pet Jokes by Michael Dahl

Spooky Sillies: A Book of Ghost Jokes by Mark Moore

Wacky Wheelies: A Book of Transportation Jokes by Mark Ziegler

Wacky Workers: A Book of Job Jokes by Mark Ziegler

What's up, Doc? A Book of Doctor Jokes by Mark Ziegler

Looking for a specific title or level? A complete list
of *Read-it!* Readers is available on our Web site:
www.picturewindowbooks.com